Herbie breathed easier. Everything was secured now. As he walked back up the stairs and across the attic, he heard a growling sound.

"Hamburger Head?" Herbie called to his dog. Quickly he shined the light on the little room. The door was still closed.

Herbie slowly inched his way back to the stairs. He didn't like the sound of that growl. It was high-pitched and mean.

Just as Herbie backed up toward the steps, he saw something big and hairy jump out of the shadows . . .

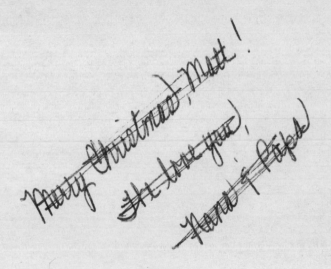

HERBIE JONES
and the Dark Attic

by Suzy Kline

ILLUSTRATED BY RICHARD WILLIAMS

SCHOLASTIC INC.

New York Toronto London Auckland Sydney
Mexico City New Delhi Hong Kong Buenos Aires

ISBN 0-439-31852-1

Text copyright © 1992 by Suzy Kline.
Illustrations copyright © 1992 by Richard Williams.
Interior artwork on pages 35, 71, and 98 by Patrick Collins. All rights reserved. Published by Scholastic Inc., 555 Broadway, New York, NY 10012, by arrangement with Puffin Books, a division of Penguin Putnam Inc. SCHOLASTIC and associated logos are trademarks and/or registered trademarks of Scholastic Inc.

12 11 10 9 8 7 6 5 4 3 2   2 3 4 5 6/0

Printed in the U.S.A.   40

First Scholastic printing, October 2001

For Charla Pinkham
my dear friend for over thirty years.

Acknowledgments

Special appreciation to . . .

The raccoon that visited our attic
and inspired this story. (He's alive
and well down by the river.)

Paul Rego, wildlife biologist, the
Connecticut Department of Environment
Protection, and the Nuisance Wildlife
Control licensed volunteers for
their service to the community.

My editor, Anne O'Connell, for her
thoughtful hard work and encouragement.

Two special librarians for their inspirations:
Bernice "Bunny" Yesner and
her collection of pencil erasers
that she displays in her hairdo.

Pam Rinaldi and her suggestions
that Annabelle be a library helper
and remind people about overdue books.

John F. Love's, *McDonalds Behind
the Arches*, Bantam Books, NY 1986,
for its fascinating facts.

And to my husband, Rufus, who thought
of the book that would finally turn
Raymond on to reading:
History of the American Hamburger.

Contents

Contents

1

The Late Phone Call

Herbie Jones couldn't sleep. When he looked at his lighted clock, it said 10:45 P.M. His dog, Hamburger Head, was stretched out on his bed with all four legs in the air.

Herbie smiled. Then he thought about school.

Tomorrow was the first day of fourth grade. But there was nothing new about it. Miss Pinkham, his third-grade teacher, was teaching fourth grade this year. Most of the kids from his third-grade class were going to be in his fourth grade class.

No surprises.

No excitement.

Herbie turned on the light and started reading his book, *The Adventures of Tom Sawyer*. Ten minutes later the phone rang. Who would be calling at eleven o'clock? Herbie wondered.

He threw back the covers and dashed into the kitchen.

By the time he got to the phone, his mother and sister were peeking around the corner in their long nightgowns. His sister, Olivia, had white splotches all over her face. Herbie knew about her night cream for pimples.

"Hello? Granddad! How are you? No, it's not five o'clock. It's eleven o'clock. We're three hours *ahead* of California. That's okay. What's up?"

As Herbie listened, his eyes got bigger. "No kidding? A THOUSAND DOLLARS?"

Olivia tried to put her ear next to the phone, but Herbie pushed her away. He didn't want any of that white goop on him.

"Really? Uh huh . . . yeah . . . uh huh . . . Oh . . . Great! Yeah, I'll have Dad call you when he gets home from his night shift. I love you, too."

As soon as Herbie hung up, his mother and

sister quizzed him. "What did Granddad want?"

"He could have gone anywhere," Herbie replied half in a daze. "The South Sea islands . . . Timbuktu . . ."

"WHERE'S HE GOING?" they asked.

"He's coming here."

"*When*?"

"Sunday."

"How did he get the thousand dollars?" Mrs. Jones asked.

"At the horse races? The lottery? Fishing derby?" Olivia was having fun guessing.

Herbie made a face. "The hospital overcharged him for his ingrown toenail surgery."

"Oh," Mrs. Jones replied. "Well, that's nice he wants to visit his family. Your dad will be glad to see his father. How long is he staying?"

"Two weeks. And he said he'll buy all the groceries." Herbie took an oatmeal cookie from the cookie jar and poured himself some milk. The conversation was getting boring.

"Your dad will be happy about that. There won't be any extra bills."

3

"Looks like everything is under control . . . except this HUGE pimple on my chin," Olivia complained. "I'm going back to bed. Tomorrow's my first day at high school and I need my beauty rest."

"Good night, dear. We can talk about your giving up your bedroom to Granddad tomorrow. I'm sure you won't mind the attic room for two short weeks."

Olivia abruptly turned around. "Move out of *my room*? Mom, you can't ask me to do that. I just paid to have my new pink telephone installed after a *long* summer of baby-sitting. I can't have Granddad taking my messages. When that phone rings, *I* want to be in *my* room to get it!"

Herbie used his arm to wipe some milk off his lips. "I'll sleep up there! Neato! It'll be like a fort. A secret fort. And dark . . . like that cave Tom Sawyer explores. I've been asking you for years, Mom, to sleep up there. Yeah! YEAH!"

"Just a minute, Herbie. Do you think you're old enough?"

"Mom, I'm a fourth-grader now. I'm not

afraid of the dark. Do you see any night-light in my room?"

Olivia yawned. "I think he can handle it, Mother."

Herbie knew Olivia just wanted to keep her own room, but his mom could make him sleep on the couch or in a sleeping bag on the floor. Herbie appreciated his sister's vote of confidence.

"Well . . ." Mrs. Jones hedged. "It's just two weeks. I guess it'll be okay."

Herbie threw his arms around his mother and gave her a big hug.

Now he was starting the school year with some excitement. Who knows what surprises there might be in the attic? Herbie thought.

2

The Dark Attic

After his mom and sister went back to bed, Herbie opened the kitchen door and tiptoed out into the hallway. He could feel a cool breeze from the back door. His dad had left it open again. Herbie's dog chewed on his pajama leg. "Come on, Hamburger Head, let's take a look at our new place!"

As the two walked across the hall to the attic stairway, Hamburger Head started to growl. Herbie turned and scolded him. "You've got to get over your dumb fear of the attic. Ever since you got your paw caught in that mousetrap last month, you haven't been up there. Well, you and I are moving up to the attic, Burger Brain, so let's get going."

When Herbie got to the top of the stairs, he felt around for the dangling chain that was attached to a naked light bulb on the wooden ceiling. As soon as he pulled on it, he looked back at his dog. Hamburger Head was sitting on the fourth step, wagging his tail. He wasn't going any farther.

Herbie scowled, then he turned and looked at the large attic. Whoa . . . he thought. There were so many shadows! Some were even weird. One looked like a witch stirring a caldron. Another resembled a big casket.

Herbie decided to get his dad's yellow flashlight on the ledge. Just as he reached for it, Herbie felt something sticky touch his face. "AAAAuuuugh!" He cringed. Then he discovered it was just a cobweb and brushed it away.

As Herbie picked up the flashlight, he felt something crawl across his hand and up his arm. Herbie shivered. Quickly he shined the light on his arm. It was a daddy longlegs.

Herbie couldn't remember ever being afraid of little things like cobwebs and insects before. He always thought they were interesting. But tonight, in the dark attic, they seemed spooky. Herbie shined the light at the far end of the attic. There was the little room his uncle stayed in all summer. Herbie noticed the door was ajar. It was just wide enough for a mouse or . . . a rat to go through.

Herbie remembered one summer evening when his uncle found a water rat in the attic stairway. It had wandered up from the river behind his house. It was huge and ugly. As his uncle coaxed it back down the stairs with a shovel, the water rat hissed and showed its sharp teeth. Herbie shuddered as he recalled the large white rat with its long, thin, pink tail.

Herbie decided not to do any more exploring in the dark alone. Just as he turned, he heard something move behind the casket shadow. And growl.

Herbie managed a small smile. "Okay, Burger Brain, I know that's you. Let's go!"

When he got to the stairwell, Herbie turned and froze. There was Hamburger Head, still sitting on the fourth step. "YYYYYYYIKES! It *wasn't* you!"

Herbie's high-pitched voice startled Hamburger Head. The dog took one flying leap over the four attic steps and flew into the kitchen, clawing and slipping on the shiny floor.

Herbie took off too.

As soon as he got back to his bedroom, Herbie leaned against the door. His heart was still racing and he was out of breath. Maybe I imagined the growling, Herbie thought. Didn't a daddy longlegs just scare him? The dark attic played tricks on his imagination.

When Herbie looked at his bed, he could see his dog's black nose sticking out of the sheet.

"Listen, Burger Brain. I know you're hiding. We wanted a little adventure. Now we've . . . got some. I just have to . . . get used to being up there . . . in the dark. I can do it. I . . . *have* to. There's no backing out . . . now. Mom's . . . depending on me."

Then Herbie sat down on his bed and wrote a poem in his notebook.

The attic, the attic
It's dark and spooky,
I've gotta be tough like Tom
I'll deal with the noises
The shadows and rattles
And after the battles
I'll eat sa-lom
Mi.

3

A Lion in the
Classroom

The next morning Miss Pinkham welcomed the class to fourth grade and started a conversation. Raymond Martin blurted out the first news. "Herbie Jones has his own apartment this year."

Herbie rolled his eyeballs. Raymond was overdoing it.

"Apartment?" Miss Pinkham raised her eyebrows. "Where?"

"In my attic," Herbie explained. "It's the same room my uncle stayed in when he visited us over the summer. It has a great view." Herbie thought he'd throw that in.

"You're staying up there *alone*?" Margie asked.

Herbie crossed his fingers under his desk. "There's nothing in my attic but a few shadows and creaky noises. That's all. Besides, I'm just staying up there for two weeks while Granddad visits."

Ray agreed. "Herbie's attic is no bogeyland. I know. I've seen *The March of the Wooden Soldiers* with Laurel and Hardy on TV."

Miss Pinkham started to laugh.

Herbie didn't think it was funny. Last night when he saw the dark attic it *looked* like a *bogeyland*! He just hoped he could muster up enough courage in four days to sleep up there.

Ten minutes later a lady twice the size of Miss Pinkham showed up at the door. Herbie noticed the two long pencils that were sticking out of her head. When she turned to chat with Miss Pinkham, he saw the big black bun that was knotted in the back of her hair. The long pencils had dangly erasers on them. One was a spider and the other was a skeleton.

"Who's that?" Ray asked.

Herbie shrugged. He had never seen her before.

Then Annabelle Louisa Hodgekiss whispered, "I know her. She's the new librarian. I met her yesterday when I dropped by the school. She said she was going to have a library helper from each room. I'm hoping it'll be me. *I'd* get people to return their library books."

Herbie gritted his teeth. That's all he needed was the Annabelle patrol in fourth grade.

"Raymond," Annabelle said as she turned around. "I noticed *your* name was on her overdue list. You've had a book out since last spring! It's called *Watch Out for These Weirdos*."

"Oh, yeah," Ray replied. "I liked that book. There were lots of neat pictures and not many words. Rhyming stuff like, 'This is Sue who belongs in the zoo,' and 'This is Annabelle who's a big fat tattletale.'"

"Raymond Martin, you know very well that's *not* how it goes! You better return that book right away. You don't know the new librarian. When she talked about overdue books, she growled and snarled like . . . a LION!"

Raymond jerked back in his seat. "Okay! I'll look for it."

"Boys and girls!" Miss Pinkham announced, "Meet Mrs. Reed, our new librarian."

Everyone stared at the erasers that were attached to the pencils in her hair. The skeleton's limbs and spider's legs were dangling and bouncing in midair.

"I'm so happy to be at Laurel Woods Elementary School. I've heard there are lots of wonderful readers here."

Miss Pinkham's class clapped.

"I want to announce the new hours. The library will be open one hour before school and one hour after school, so if you want to stop by and check out books then, you may."

"Do you like spiders?" Herbie asked.

Mrs. Reed pulled the spider pencil out of her hair. "I'm glad you asked . . . eh . . ."

"Herbie Jones."

"Well, Herbie, I have a special display in the

library about spiders. I just got a new shipment of books in."

Herbie smiled. He liked insects and Mrs. Reed.

Annabelle raised her hand. "What if you have an overdue book?" Then she looked back at Raymond.

Ray slowly sank down in his chair while the librarian made a lion face. "Grrrrrrr . . . GRRRRRRR!"

The class turned pin quiet. Ray ducked under his desk.

"*That's* what I think of overdue books."

"We're looking forward to our weekly visit to the library," Miss Pinkham replied.

Herbie tried not to laugh at his buddy, who kept pretending to tie his shoe under his desk. Herbie remembered the growling that spooked *him* last night. Fears weren't funny.

"Before I go," Mrs. Reed added, "I want the library helper from this room to pass out these new bookmarks."

Annabelle started to stand up.

"Margie Sherman?" Mrs. Reed called.

Margie jumped out of her chair. "Me?"

"Please pass these out, and then stop by the library sometime to see me."

"Yes, Mrs. Reed." Margie looked at her best friend, Annabelle, and beamed, but Annabelle just looked straight ahead, folded her arms, and flared her nostrils.

It looked to Herbie like Margie was in for Annabelle's silent treatment.

When Ray finally sat up in his seat, he whispered to his buddy, "W-will you h-help me look for that WEIRDO b-book?"

Herbie gave his pal the A-okay sign. And then he thought about fourth grade. It had gotten off to a scary start all right. For him *and* for Raymond.

4

The Accident

When the class had finished sharing their summer news, Miss Pinkham announced the reading groups.

Annabelle's face turned white as she reread the names on the yellow chart. "I'm with Raymond Martin and Herbie Jones? There must be some mistake."

Herbie couldn't believe it either. Everyone knew that Annabelle was the smartest person in the class and Ray was the slowest.

"This year," Miss Pinkham explained, "your group will choose books to read, talk about them, and then do projects together."

"But that's not fair," Annabelle complained. "You put your best students with . . ." Annabelle bit her lip. She wanted to choose the appropriate words. ". . . with those students who haven't reached their potential yet." And then she glared at Herbie and Raymond.

"In fourth grade," Miss Pinkham said, "everyone will have to do his share. Or the group will suffer. If you help each other out, your group will do well."

Annabelle started scribbling dark circles on her notepad.

"Today when you meet for the first time, you might want to think of a name for your group and then talk about your summer reading for a while. Any questions?"

Ray was clasping his hands in the air. He and Herbie were together.

"Now," the teacher directed, "take your chairs to one corner of the room, carefully."

Everyone got up and started moving. The noise was so loud, Miss Pinkham closed the classroom door. Annabelle pointed to the window with the potted marigolds. "Let's meet over in that corner," she ordered.

Jose Fernandez, Sarah Sitwellington, and

Herbie got there first. They made a half circle with their chairs and sat down. Annabelle supervised Ray's progress across the room. "Raymond Martin," she scolded, "you don't carry your chair over your head. You could hurt someone. Carry it like this, next to your chest."

Just as she turned to the window, she hit Herbie's face with her chair.

Blood spurted from his mouth and Sarah shrieked. "EWEYEE! LOOK!"

"HERBIE'S BLEEDING!" Jose shouted.

Miss Pinkham ran over to Herbie. "My goodness! What happened to you?"

Ray pointed to Annabelle. "Captain Boss here wasn't looking where she was going. She clobbered Herbie right in the face with her chair."

Annabelle put her head down. "I didn't mean to. It was . . . an accident."

Herbie glared at her. "Next time look where you're going!"

"Eweyee," Sarah replied. "Herbie dribbles blood when he talks."

21

Miss Pinkham grabbed some tissues from her desk. "Open your mouth, Herbie," she said, dabbing his lip.

The children huddled around and watched as Herbie showed his teeth, tongue, and throat.

"Oh no!" Margie exclaimed, "what if Herbie had his teeth knocked out?"

"He'd have to wear false teeth like my dad," Ray replied. "You have to soak those choppers every night in a glass of guck."

Annabelle covered her eyes and cringed.

Miss Pinkham sighed. "Your teeth are fine, Herbie, but I'm sending you to the nurse. She may want you to go to the emergency room to see if you need stitches."

"Stitches?" Herbie replied. He didn't like the idea of someone putting a needle in his lip.

Ray patted his buddy on the back. "You can handle it. One or two stitches is nothing. Look at Frankenstein. That guy had thousands of stitches and he got around just fine."

As Herbie walked down the hall to the

nurse's office, he thought about his buddy, Raymond. Ray loved spooky stuff like monster movies and spying in the dark. He wasn't afraid of anything spooky, just a librarian.

Maybe Ray could spend the first night with him in the attic.

5

The Emergency Room

Ten minutes later Mr. Jones picked Herbie up at the nurse's office and drove him to the Laurel Woods Hospital emergency room. As they sat in the waiting room, Mr. Jones eyeballed his son's lip. "That thing's as fat as the donuts at your mom's restaurant."

"Funny," Herbie grumbled.

"Well, son, if my factory medical insurance wasn't paying for this, I'd be grumbling along with you. So you're all set to move up to the attic?"

That was also a sore subject, Herbie thought. His big mouth got him in that too! "Uh huh."

"Good. You can move up there tonight."

"TONIGHT? Ouch!" When Herbie jerked, he hurt his lip.

"I want to freshen up the woodwork around your bedroom windows with some white paint. Make it nice for Pops. Okay with you?"

"Yeah . . . sure." Then Herbie rolled his eyeballs. Tonight? He wasn't ready. It was supposed to be Sunday, when he had gained more courage. He could talk about it with Ray when he got back to school. Thinking about the attic *now* just made matters worse. Herbie had to get his mind on something that wasn't scary.

Quickly he surveyed the room and tried to guess why people were there. The first two were obvious. One man was coughing in the corner. The boy sitting next to him had an arm in a sling.

When Herbie looked at the little redheaded girl across from him, she looked fine. Her mother knew Herbie was curious. "My daughter put two peanuts up her nose."

Herbie cringed. Then he smiled at the little

girl. As soon as she saw Herbie's bloody teeth, she started to cry.

Herbie quickly covered his mouth.

And then the mother shrieked. "THEY FELL OUT!"

Herbie and his dad looked at the little girl with her runny nose. There, on her white blouse, were two wet peanuts.

"Thank you so much, young man!" the lady said as she jumped to her feet. "Maybe you'll be a doctor someday. Come on, Priscilla!"

Mr. Jones patted his son on the back. "See how helpful it is to be ugly?"

Herbie punched his dad in the shoulder.

Just then the sliding doors opened and two people rushed in. "Mrs. Von Whistle, Mr. Hodgekiss! What's the matter?" Herbie's dad asked.

Mr. Hodgekiss quickly helped the gray-haired lady to the reception desk and then walked over to Mr. Jones. "Mrs. Von Whistle was bitten by a raccoon that got trapped in her hallway. She had called me about the raccoon being a pest, and I was on my way. Unfortunately, I was too late."

Mr. Hodgekiss sat down next to Herbie. "I'm a volunteer for the Nuisance Wildlife Control in our neighborhood. Usually I get called at night. This time I was called from work. What happened to you, Herbie? Did you get in a fight the first day of school?"

"Yeah." Herbie tried not to laugh. "With your daughter."

"Annabelle hit you?"

"With a chair. It was an accident in our reading group."

"She's not a very charming chairman, is she?"

Herbie smiled. He liked Mr. Hodgekiss's sense of humor.

Mr. Hodgekiss examined Herbie's lip. "Are you okay?"

"Yeah, but I might need some stitches. How about Mrs. Von Whistle?"

"She'll be okay, too, but we have to find that raccoon. It's on the loose in our neighborhood."

"I always thought raccoons made good pets," Mr. Jones said.

"They can be when they're young," Mr. Hodgekiss replied. "But older ones get pretty bad tempered. If they come down with a virus, they can become rabid."

"Rabid?" Herbie wasn't sure of the word.

"That's when the raccoon has rabies," Mr. Hodgekiss explained.

Herbie got goose pimples just thinking about it. When the nurse suddenly called his name, Herbie was so jittery he jumped out of his seat. He didn't like the idea of stitches either.

6

Raccoons and
Mrs. Reed

When Herbie returned to school at lunch recess, everyone on the playground ran over to greet him.

"Are you okay, partner?" Ray asked, looking at the one large bandage on his lip.

"Yeah. I just needed two stitches. It didn't even hurt. Dr. Huckaby gave me something for it."

Annabelle pushed her way through the crowd. After she looked at Herbie's bandage, she started to whisper, "I'm . . ."

Herbie knew Annabelle hardly ever apologized. He wanted everyone to hear it. "Huh? What did you say?"

Annabelle knew the bell was going to ring

any minute so she waited. Just as it went off, she shouted, "I'M SORRY!"

The crowd ran back to the building.

Herbie shook his head. He knew they didn't hear her.

Miss Pinkham noticed Herbie right away. "I'm glad you're back!"

"Me too," Herbie replied. "That emergency room was full of bad news. One of my neighbors got bit by a raccoon. Annabelle's father was there helping her."

"Oh, no!" Miss Pinkham replied.

"If anyone here sees a raccoon, don't go near it," Herbie warned. "Just call the wildlife hotline."

Annabelle raised her hand. "If there's a problem in our Laurel Woods area, my father gets called. He's a licensed volunteer for the Nuisance Wildlife Control. Dad said there are more than two thousand raccoon cases reported in Connecticut a year."

Miss Pinkham put down her math book and listened.

"Sometimes my dad is called to help a neighbor get a snake out of the patio, or a gray squirrel in a basement, or a bat in an attic."

Herbie closed his eyes. The thought of a bat in the attic gave him the willies.

"What does he do with those pests?" John Creenweed asked.

"He puts them back safely in nature."

Miss Pinkham folded her arms. "I think we'll postpone our lesson on fractions. Margie, please go to the library and ask Mrs. Reed for all the books she has on raccoons."

"Yes, Miss Pinkham." Just as Margie looked over at Annabelle and smiled, Annabelle flared her nostrils at her.

"Here's the *R* encyclopedia," Miss Pinkham said as she pulled it from the bookshelf in the classroom. "I'll read you some information about the raccoon."

Herbie looked over at Ray. He was paying attention.

"The raccoon is related to the panda bear," Miss Pinkham read. "He's a mammal with a pointed, black-tipped nose, a black mask marking, and a bushy tail ringed in buff and black. Does anyone know the color of buff?"

Annabelle's hand went up first. "It's the color of leather, light yellow-brown."

"Very good, Annabelle. Now, class, while we are waiting for our books about raccoons, let's try sketching one. Jose, please pass out white paper."

As soon as everyone was ready, the teacher began drawing the face of a raccoon on the chalkboard. The students worked hard on their drawings. From time to time Miss Pinkham would check the *R* encyclopedia for details.

"Look at mine," Raymond shouted as he held his up.

Just then Mrs. Reed and Margie appeared at the door. Their hands were full of books. "Is this the animal research center?" the librarian asked.

Miss Pinkham laughed. "It sure is. Show Mrs. Reed your pictures, class."

Everyone held up their raccoons.

"Oh, my goodness," Mrs. Reed exclaimed.

"And now, thanks to you," Miss Pinkham said, "the children can find more interesting facts about raccoons."

"Great," Mrs. Reed replied.

As they passed out the books, Mrs. Reed noticed the name tag on Ray's desk. "Hmm. Raymond Martin. I know that name. Did you know you have a book checked out that is five months overdue?"

Ray looked into the librarian's pupils. He thought they were as big as bowling balls.

"Y—yes."

"Are you going to start looking for it?"

Ray moved his head sideways as he watched her skeleton eraser dance back and forth.

"Are you shaking your head to tell me no? Grrrrrrr . . . GRRRRRR!"

Ray sat up. "I mean yes. YES! I'll bring it in tomorrow."

Mrs. Reed put a raccoon book on Ray's desk and smiled. "Share this with a friend."

Ray wanted to smile back but he was too afraid.

Herbie saw the whole thing. He would help his buddy find that book before class tomorrow. Right now, Ray had to help *him*!

7

Frankenstein
to the Rescue

"How's your lip?" Olivia asked when Herbie and Ray walked in the house. She was on the phone but was able to stretch the cord a few feet into the living room.

"It's okay."

Mrs. Jones, who came home early from Dipping Donuts, rushed over to Herbie and peeked under the bandage. "Two stitches! Are they sore, dear?"

Herbie normally wouldn't have complained, but he had a favor to ask, so he thought mentioning the pain might be helpful.

"They pinch a little when I smile. Eh . . . Mom?"

"What is it?"

"Can Raymond sleep over? We have a lot of homework and we wanted to do it together."

"But it's a school night, boys," Mrs. Jones replied.

Mr. Jones stepped into the living room. He had a paintbrush in his hand and a white cap on his head. "It might be a good idea since this is Herbie's first night up in the attic. He might like some company."

"Yeah!" Herbie replied.

"I left some purple paint and brushes behind the attic door. If you want to, you can decorate your walls sometime."

"Thanks, Dad." Herbie looked at his mom. She was still thinking.

"This would *not* be your usual Saturday night sleepover, boys. Bedtime would be a lot earlier, and I would expect you to go to sleep so you can get your rest."

Herbie and Ray nodded their heads.

"Would your mother let you stay, Raymond?"

"She already said yes," Ray replied as he

held up his night bag. Herbie jabbed his buddy.

Mrs. Jones laughed. "Well, all right, then. Let me go upstairs and clean things up a bit. I want to vacuum and change the sheets. You boys can get started on your homework right away and then we'll go out to dinner."

"Go OUT to dinner?" Herbie and Ray repeated.

Mr. Jones stuck his head around the bedroom door again. "Who's paying?"

"Where are we going?" Olivia asked as she pulled on the phone cord. "I don't want to see anyone I know with this huge zit on my chin."

Mrs. Jones held her hand up. "I thought we'd use these three Burger Paradise coupons. You know, Buy one cheeseburger, get one free."

Ray started to drool. "CHEESEBURGERS!"

"No drinks?" Olivia asked.

Mr. Jones tipped his painter's hat. "We'll have the cheapest and finest drink made for man. Adam and Eve's favorite."

"ADAM'S ALE," Herbie and Raymond replied.

"Water." Olivia groaned. She'd heard her dad joke about that before.

"Except for Herbie," Mr. Jones replied. "He gets a milk shake. He can't eat any solids today. Doctor's orders."

Herbie grumbled a few words as he and Ray headed for the kitchen table. He had forgotten about the doctor's orders.

When they sat down, Ray was humming the Burger Paradise tune he heard a lot on TV.

"So what's the homework we have to do?" Ray asked. He wanted to hurry up and get it done so they could go out to eat.

Herbie handed Ray some paper and a pen. "Just write about a favorite scene in some book you've read."

"Okay." Ray started writing. "How do you spell 'Count Dracula'?"

Herbie looked up. "Ray, you didn't read about Count Dracula. You saw him on the late movie."

"So? Miss Pinkham won't know. There *are*

books about Count Dracula. I saw my dad reading them."

"Fine, Ray." Herbie wasn't going to argue. What else could Ray write about? The truth was, the only thing Ray read that *didn't* have a lot of pictures was a Burger Paradise menu. Herbie started spelling the word: "C-o-u-n-t . . ."

"Does blood have one or two *o's*?"

"Two."

"Vampire have an *e* at the end?"

Herbie put his pen down. "Ray, we're sleeping in the attic tonight, and you want to talk about spooky stuff. Come on!"

Ray pointed his pen at his buddy. "Why, Herbie Jones, you're afraid. *That's* why you wanted me to sleep over tonight. You don't want to sleep in the attic alone."

Herbie held up a tight fist. "So . . . what if I am a little afraid of the attic. It's the first night. Haven't *you* ever been afraid of something?"

Ray was quiet. "Yeah."

Herbie wondered if he was going to say, "The librarian."

"I get scared every time I have to read words

aloud in front of the class. I'm afraid they'll laugh at my mistakes."

Herbie moved his chair closer to his buddy. He felt bad about that. Herbie looked at Ray's paper. "You can read what you're writing now, can't you?"

"Yeah, but that's different. I'm choosing all the words." Suddenly Ray crunched up his paper and tossed it in the garbage. "Forget it! Miss Pinkham won't let me do this. And I don't have a Count Dracula book that I can read. My dad's book is too hard."

"Wait a minute," Herbie said. "I think I have a *Junior Illustrated Classic Comic Book* in my room."

"Comic book?" Ray smiled. "That's got lots of pictures!"

Herbie left the kitchen. In a few minutes he was back. "I don't have *Count Dracula,* but I have *Frankenstein.* Want to read this one?"

"Neato! But do you think the teacher will let me use it?"

"Sure. It's not a regular comic book. It's a

classic illustrated one. That means it's about a great book."

Ray beamed. "Want to read it with me, Herbie?"

Herbie wasn't thrilled with the choice of topic, but it was a step in the right direction. Ray was willing to do his homework about a scene from a book. Herbie figured he would just have to toughen up.

"Sure. That's why we're getting together to-night, right?" Herbie smiled even though it hurt his lip.

"Yeah," Ray bragged. "You need my help. And I"—Ray slowed his words down—"I need yours."

8

An Evening in Paradise

Two hours later, at 5:15 P.M., the boys finished their homework assignment. Herbie looked over Ray's paper. "You read that perfectly, Raymond. You even got the tough words."

"'Experiment,' 'strangle,' and 'lightning' are easy. It's those boring ones like 'their' and 'they're' that throw me."

Herbie patted his pal on the back. "It's cheeseburger time. Let's get out of here."

"YAHOO!" Ray shouted.

Just as the Jones family and Raymond were about to walk through the Burger Paradise glass door, Olivia stopped. "Oh, no! *He's* working here!"

"Who is?" Mrs. Jones asked.

"Lance Pellizini. He's the tall boy behind the counter taking orders. He's in my drama class at school. He's . . . Tom Sawyer." Olivia's dreamy voice suddenly cracked. "And I'm Aunty Polly in our play. Sylvia Newton gets to be Rebecca Thatcher. That's who he falls in love with. Oh, I'm so embarrassed. Here I am with my family and my little brother and his little friend."

"Excuse me," Herbie replied. "We're in fourth grade now. We're not little."

"Herbie's moving up to the attic," Ray snapped. "He's even got his own apartment."

"Yeah!" Herbie replied, feeling a sudden surge of power.

Olivia turned her head. "Well, *please* act your age and don't embarrass me. That goes for you, too, Dad. Everyone act casual."

When she looked at her mother, she smiled. "I know you won't embarrass me, Mom. Can you notice the pimple on my chin?"

"No, dear," Mrs. Jones said as she stepped on the doormat. Suddenly a blue light started to flash on and off.

"AAAAAAAAAAAAAaaaaaaaaaa!" blared a siren. Then a loudspeaker announced: "We just had our five-hundredth customer walk through the Paradise door. And, every time we have customer five hundred, we have the Paradise Blue Light Special! That customer and his or her guests get a free photo. Please stay where you are!"

A manager wearing a hat that said "Welcome to Paradise" came rushing over to Mrs. Jones. "Ma'am, you and your family have won a free photo. Please stand over here by the salad bar and we'll take your picture."

"I'm *dying*," Olivia whispered to her mother. "I don't believe it! Everyone in this restaurant is staring at us. Including . . . him."

Herbie and Ray looked at Lance Pellizini. He was watching.

"Over here by the onions, sir. Your wife can stand next to you. Boys either side of this lovely young lady. Now say, 'Burger Paradise.'"

"BURGER PARADISE!" Herbie and Ray shouted.

Olivia's face was as red as the cherry tomatoes when the camera flash went off.

The manager raised his arms. "Let's give this lucky family a big hand!"

Everyone clapped, including Lance Pellizini. Olivia took a quick step away from the blue spotlight, which was still flashing. Unfortunately she slipped on an onion and started to fall.

Whoooooosh! Olivia tried to land on her knee as gracefully as possible.

Herbie looked at his sister as he offered his hand. "Now that's what I call casual."

Olivia gritted her teeth. "This is the worst night of my life," she said as she pulled the onion off her kneecap. It was stuck to her skin. When she looked up, she cringed. Lance was still watching.

"Six cheeseburgers, one chocolate milk shake, and five waters," Mr. Jones said as he laid three coupons down on the counter.

Olivia looked away. Her dad was so embarrassing. Five waters, she thought.

The manager who took the picture stepped in front of Lance. "This family doesn't pay. They get our Five-hundredth-Customer Blue Light Special. They may order anything they want."

"Wow!" Ray said. "Did you hear that?"

"Huddle up!" Mr. Jones said as he put his arms around the boys and Mrs. Jones. "We have big decisions to make here. Olivia?"

Olivia refused to join them. She had had enough of family togetherness. "I'll have whatever you decide," she mumbled.

Lance stood at the counter, adjusting his white cap that said "Welcome to Paradise." Quietly he leaned over and looked at Olivia.

"Now this place really *is* paradise. *You're* here."

Olivia broke into a big smile. Then she put her hand over her chin.

Lance continued talking. "I wish you were reading the part of Rebecca Thatcher in our drama play."

"You do?"

"I sure do. Hey, maybe we could practice

our scene together. How about tonight?" Lance asked.

Olivia gulped. "We could practice at my house. Do you know where I live?"

"We studied world history together once. Remember? I get off work at seven-thirty P.M."

"I'll see you then, Lance."

"Great."

"Okay!" Mr. Jones said, rubbing his hands together. "We'll have four cheeseburgers, four french fries, four salad bars, four onion rings, four milks, four apple turnovers. And one giant chocolate milk shake."

Herbie frowned. He knew what he was getting.

As they took the five trays of food and drink to a table by the window, Olivia sighed. "Now I know I'm in paradise."

Ray popped six golden french fries into his mouth. "Me too, Olive. This *is* paradise."

Herbie made a face as he slurped on his milk shake.

9

Herbie and Ray in Bogeyland

As soon as Herbie and Ray got inside the house, they washed up and put on their pajamas. Then they headed for the attic. "'Night, everyone!"

"I'll walk you upstairs," Mrs. Jones said.

The boys made long faces.

"Mom." Herbie groaned. "We're fourth-graders now. We don't have to be tucked in."

"*No way,*" Ray agreed.

"Okay, boys. See you in the morning."

Herbie gave his mom a hug. "'NIGHT, DAD!" he called into the living room.

"'NIGHT, SON. 'NIGHT, RAY!" Mr. Jones was looking at a Fix-It-Yourself book.

Herbie started to say goodnight to Olivia but she was just turning on the vacuum cleaner.

Herbie looked at his dog sleeping soundly at the foot of his dad's chair. As soon as the vacuum roared up, Hamburger Head jumped in the air and then raced around the corner into Herbie's bedroom.

Herbie and Ray laughed. Then they headed upstairs. When they got to the top landing, they could see the light coming from the little room at the end of the attic. Herbie reached for the yellow flashlight on a side ledge and shined it around. "Okay, Ray, we have to check this place out before we settle down."

"We do?" Ray looked around. He didn't like all the shadows. "Man, we landed in bogeyland." When he saw the witch's shadow, he jumped on Herbie's back. "Aaaaaugh!"

Herbie carried Ray piggyback over to the weird shadow and shined his light. "Look, Ray! It's just a broom and coat."

Ray slowly slid down Herbie's back and boasted, "Yeah, well . . . once you know what things are, you're not afraid."

"Now we have to check that casket shadow over there."

"Eh . . . why don't we do that later, Herbie. I'm getting t-tired." Ray made a phony yawn: "Ahhhhhyaaaaaaa!"

"Ray! You said you'd *help* me."

"Ooooo keeeeee do-do-do dokey!" Ray shivered.

Herbie walked over to the side of the attic by the window. "Look! It's a big refrigerator box!"

"Yeah!" Ray said as he held on to Herbie's pajama tops. "Let's go now."

"Wait a minute, I have to check inside." Herbie decided not to mention the growling he had heard the other night.

Slowly, Herbie knelt down and shined the flashlight around. "I don't see anything." Then when he put his hand inside, he felt something sharp. "Aaaaugh!" Herbie jerked back.

Ray jumped on Herbie's back again. "Wh-what?"

Herbie held out his hand. "It's just some cardboard dividers. Would you get off me!"

"Whoa!" Ray said, wiping the sweat off his forehead. "I bet you're glad I'm up here with you!"

Herbie made a face. "Okay, Captain Coura-
geous, we checked all the bad spots. It looks
okay now." Just as the boys were walking by
the attic window, they felt something scratchy
touch their faces. Both boys ran to the attic
room and closed the door.

"It . . . was just . . . the . . . lacy . . . cur-
tain," Herbie replied. While he was getting his
breath back, he looked around the room. The
bed was folded down and the rug was vacuumed. His mother had even put a bouquet of
daisies on the little table by the window. As
Herbie looked out onto the street, he could see
the leafy branches of the maple tree and hear
Olivia's vacuum below.

"This place really could be neat," Herbie replied, "if . . . it wasn't for the rest of the dark
attic."

"Look who's coming up the walk," Ray said
as he pressed his nose against the window.
"That Lance guy."

"Yeah, they're practicing their lines from
Tom Sawyer. It's a good book. You want me to
read you a chapter or two?"

Ray smiled. "Yeah. I saw the movie on TV. It was great!"

As the boys settled into bed, Ray listened to Herbie read about Aunt Polly chasing Tom with a broom, Tom painting the white fence, and Tom getting enough tickets at Sunday School for a Bible. When they got to the school scene where Tom told Becky he loved her, Ray threw his head back on the pillow. "Aaaauuugh, it's getting deadly. Don't read me any more."

And then Herbie stopped suddenly. "Shhhhh. I hear something."

Ray sat up. "What?"

"Shhhhhh!"

The boys listened.

"I hear it!" Ray said. "Something's out there!" Then he hid under the covers.

Herbie walked slowly toward the door. "It's . . . probably Mom checking on us."

Ray brought the sheet down over his eyes. "Yeah?"

Herbie opened the door and called, "Mom?"

There was no answer.

"It's the bogeyman!" Ray said as he shivered under the sheets.

"Ray! It's probably . . . Hamburger Head. My dog! That's it."

Ray pulled back the sheet. "I bet it is, too!"

Herbie felt a little guilty. He knew his dog didn't like the attic, but it was a possibility, and it did get Ray up.

"Okay, let's just check it out."

The boys tiptoed outside the little room. "It sounds like the noise is behind the refrigerator box," Herbie said, pointing his flashlight.

"Y-you m-mean the c-c-casket sh-shadow?"

"It'll be . . . okay, Ray," Herbie said. The boys crept over to the box. Just as Herbie shined the light on the other side and saw what was making the noise, he leaped three feet in the air. "AAAAAaaaauuuuuuGGG!"

Ray raced back to the room, slammed the door, and hid under the bed.

Herbie couldn't move. He was too shocked. *There* were his sister and Lance behind the box. Kissing!

As soon as they saw Herbie, they both screamed and jumped.

Mr. and Mrs. Jones came storming up the attic stairs. Hamburger Head barked from the bottom step.

Olivia and Lance quickly smoothed their hair. Herbie could tell they were very embarrassed.

"WHAT'S GOING ON UP HERE?" Mr. Jones bellowed.

Herbie glanced at his sister. She looked like she was going to cry. Lance just looked uncomfortable. He put both hands in his jeans pockets and stared at the wooden floor.

"Eh, here it is," Herbie replied, walking over to the witch shadow. "They were looking for a broom for their Tom Sawyer skit."

Olivia sighed with relief. "Y-yes! Thanks, Herbie. We were having a hard time finding it."

Lance took his hand out of his pocket and pointed at Olivia. "She has to hit me in the rear end with a broom for our play." He was trying to be funny.

But no one laughed.

"Well, let's all go back downstairs so the boys can get some sleep," Mr. Jones grumbled.

Olivia looked at her brother and pantomimed the word THANKS.

Herbie nodded. As he headed back to the little room, he felt much better. It was over. He knew what the strange noises were.

When he got inside the room, Ray crawled out from under the bed.

Herbie set the flashlight on the table. "Don't worry, Ray, it wasn't the bogeyman."

Ray sat down on the bed. "Who was it?"

"Lance and Olivia."

"Oh. What were *they* doing in the attic?"

Herbie couldn't say the *k* word. He had to spell it. "They were k-i-s-s-i-n-g."

"AAAUUUUUUGH!" Ray buried his head under his pillow. "Give me the bogeyman anytime!"

10

Looking for Weirdos

The next morning the boys walked to school like heroes.

"Well, *we* did it!" Herbie said. "Now *I* just have to do it myself, tonight. *Alone.*" Herbie suddenly had a long face.

"You'll be fine," Ray replied. "Just remember what the scariest thing in bogeyland was . . ."

". . . my sister!"

The boys cracked up.

Then they noticed Annabelle was ahead of them, and Margie was across the street. Both girls looked straight ahead.

"Don't you think it's dumb not to talk to someone?" Ray said.

"Yes," Herbie agreed. "Very dumb. My Sunday School teacher says you shouldn't stay angry all day. That's what the Bible says."

"It makes sense," Ray replied. "Just look at Margie and Annabelle. They have prune faces. They refuse to smile. Let's blast 'em out with that 'Take Me Out to the Ballgame' song that your uncle taught us last summer."

When Ray started humming the tune, Herbie thought it would be fun to make up their own lyrics.

"Take me out for a burrrrrger
Take me out for a Coke
Buy me some french fries and onion rings
We can't help it if we're always broke!"

Ray clapped. "Now that's gonna be my favorite song. Let's sing it together!"

As the boys sang their burger song, Annabelle and Margie looked back and laughed. When the girls looked at each other, they immediately changed their smiles to frowns and continued walking down their separate sides of the street.

The boys shook their heads.

When they came to Ray's house, Herbie stopped singing. "Now listen, we don't have much time to find that Weirdo book, so we have to think of possible places that it might be. Any ideas?"

Ray stepped over his dog, Shadow. He was sleeping in the doorway.

"I don't know . . . This may be our toughest spy case, Herbie. Those Weirdos go back five months."

"Do you remember where you were when you were reading it?"

"I was in third grade. Come on!"

"Hmmm." Herbie tried to think like a detective as they walked into Ray's dark house. The curtains were drawn as usual, and the coffee table was heaped high with stuff—a pile of letters, magazines, and a pizza box stained with sauce. When Herbie peeked under the cover, he saw a piece of pepperoni pizza all shriveled up.

"Your Weirdo book isn't here," he said.

When Herbie looked out the backyard window, he saw Mrs. Martin painting a picture of their old barn in the morning sun. "Your mom is a great artist, Ray."

"Yeah, but I can draw Viking ships better, and she can't do Count Dracula."

Herbie nodded.

For the next ten minutes the boys looked under tables, the couch, Ray's bed, in closets, and behind desks. No Weirdos.

They were about to give up when Mrs. Martin came in the house. She had paint on her face and hands. As soon as she saw Ray she gave him a kiss on the forehead.

"*Mom . . .*"

Mrs. Martin smiled at Herbie while she wiped a paint smudge off Ray's face. "I didn't know you boys were stopping by here before school. Forget something?"

Raymond groaned. "We're looking for something I lost last April."

"What is it?"

"An old library book," Ray said.

Mrs. Martin rubbed her forehead with her long shirtsleeve. "Let's see. I usually put things that are important in places where they don't get lost."

Suddenly Ray clicked his fingers. "I got it! It's where you keep our red address book."

"THE REFRIGERATOR!" Mrs. Martin and Ray shouted.

The three of them ran into the kitchen and opened it up. There was the address book on the wire rack next to a package of liver and a jar of pickled beet slices.

Ray put his hands on his head. "It's all coming back to my brain now. I remember I was thinking about library day. I was afraid I might forget so I put it . . . UNDERNEATH THIS!"

Mrs. Martin's and Herbie's eyes were as big as the beet slices. There was the book, *Watch Out for These Weirdos*, sitting at the bottom of the refrigerator under the vegetable crisper.

"This is my lucky day!" Ray shouted. "Let's hit the road!"

Herbie and Ray dashed out the door and jumped over Shadow.

When they got to school, they were out of

breath. "We've got five minutes before the bell rings," Herbie said.

The boys walked into the library. "Where is she?" Herbie whispered.

Ray looked around. When he spotted two pencils with elephant erasers bobbing around the top of the bookshelf, he knew it was her.

"Mrs. Reed?" Ray said.

The librarian stepped out from behind the bookshelf. "Well, hello, boys. It's nice to have some morning customers. I don't think the word's out yet to all the parents that I'm open for business before and after school."

"Here's the Weirdo book," Ray said proudly.

Mrs. Reed smiled as she reached for it. "My! This is a cold book."

Ray looked away. He decided not to tell the librarian where it had been. Quickly he walked over to Herbie, who was busy looking at the spider display. "Let's get out of here," Ray whispered.

"Just a minute. I want to check out one of these books," Herbie replied.

"I might have a book for you, Raymond," Mrs. Reed said as she joined the boys.

"I don't think so," Ray moaned. "I don't like to read."

"Did you see this one? I just got it last week."

Ray casually looked up. When he saw the book, he shouted, "YAHOO!"

Herbie turned around immediately and read the title: *History of the American Hamburger*.

"It has lots of pictures," Mrs. Reed said, "and interesting facts. Did you know that there is a Hamburger University?"

"No kidding?" Ray was drooling. "I never thought I wanted to go to college before, but now I might change my mind."

"Restaurant managers who open McDonald's go there."

Ray took a quick look at the pictures inside and then the glossy cover of a giant cheeseburger. "Can I check this out?"

"Sure, your record is clean," Mrs. Reed said, taking a pencil out of her hair. "Or should I say 'cool'?"

Herbie laughed.

Ray wasn't sure if the librarian was mad or not. He didn't think librarians cracked jokes like he and Herbie did.

After they checked out their books, he asked Mrs. Reed a question. "How did you know I love hamburgers?"

"Well, Raymond," Mrs. Reed said, "a librarian knows where to get information. It's my job. I just looked up Raymond Martin in the *M* encyclopedia and it said, 'Raymond Martin loves hamburgers.'"

Ray knew she was joking now, and he wasn't afraid to laugh.

As the boys were walking out, Ray called back, "Let me know when *History of French Fries* comes in."

11

Cheeseburgers

That day in class, Herbie's reading group met. Annabelle and Margie were sitting at opposite ends of the circle. Ray had his book, *History of the American Hamburger*, on his lap.

"We don't have a name. We haven't picked out the book we want to read, we haven't started a project!" Annabelle complained as she twisted one of her permed curls.

Ray held up his book. "Here's our answer."

Annabelle looked at the glossy picture on the cover and laughed. "You got a book on cheeseburgers?"

Jose and Sarah looked over Ray's shoulders. "Did you know," Ray continued, "that if you lined up all the hamburgers McDonald's sold you could go to the moon and back?"

The group ooohed and aahhed.

"And if you took all the ketchup they use, you could fill the Mississippi River with it?"

Annabelle raised her eyebrows. "Did you read those facts yourself?"

"I read the first two chapters this morning in class. It's great stuff."

Annabelle seized the opportunity. "Raymond Martin, *if* we decide to use your book, would you promise to do your share of the work in our group? That includes homework."

"If it's about hamburgers or french fries, I'll work hard."

Jose and Herbie laughed.

Annabelle started to flare her nostrils, then she stopped. "Well, it's a beginning. Now, all in favor of reading *History of the American Hamburger* please raise your hand."

Everyone raised his hand.

"It's unanimous," Annabelle said. "If we took turns reading it aloud and showing the pictures in group today, maybe we could start our project after school tomorrow."

"We could make a chart of all those great facts about hamburgers," Jose suggested.

"We could meet in my attic room," Herbie said.

"You mean your apartment?" Margie teased.

"Yeah!"

"Is it well lighted and ventilated?" Annabelle quizzed. "And is there enough room for us to work?"

"Sure."

"I'll ask Mom if I can bring cookies," Sarah said.

"Okay," Annabelle replied. "We'll meet in Herbie's room tomorrow after school. Boys, why don't you go to the supply table and get some chart paper, Magic Markers, and white art paper."

When the boys left and the circle turned quiet, Margie tried to break the uncomfortable silence. "I just finished sketching a poster for the library. See? It says, YOU CAN READ

ANYWHERE. Do you want to help me color in the sky?"

Annabelle glanced at the poster. "If that girl were *really* reading on the moon, she'd be wearing a space suit with an oxygen tank. How can that girl breathe? The picture doesn't make sense."

Margie brushed away a tear.

"I like it," Sarah replied. "It has lots of imagination and that Big Dipper is fun. I'll help you color in the sky, Margie."

When the boys returned to the group, Margie was blowing her nose.

"Our first meeting tomorrow is going to be *neato*," Ray said with a toothy smile.

Margie put her head down. She was wondering when Annabelle was going to stop being mean to her.

Herbie looked up at the clock. He was hoping he would have enough courage to sleep in the attic alone tonight.

12

Herbie's Night in the Attic

"Are you sure you don't want me to walk you upstairs?" Mrs. Jones said.

"No, Mom. I'll see you in the morning. Thanks for the flowers and clean room."

Mrs. Jones hugged her son.

"GOOD NIGHT, DAD. GOOD NIGHT, OLIVE," Herbie shouted. Mr. Jones was painting and Olivia was doing her homework.

"'NIGHT, HERBIE!" they called back.

"Come on, Hamburger Head, we're sleeping up in the attic." The dog got up from the doorway, stretched, and followed Herbie out the kitchen door.

When Herbie got to the top of the stairs, Hamburger Head refused to go any farther.

"Okay, Burger Brain. I'll carry you." Quickly he walked across the attic floor. Herbie thought his dog's heart was beating as fast as his. "We're going to do this, Hamburger Head. But first we'll get some help."

As soon as he got inside the little room, Herbie closed the door tightly and knelt by his bed.

"Dear God, I would feel a lot better if you would spend the night with me up here in the attic. I can go through the tough times if you're with me. Bless Mom, Dad, Olive, Hamburger Head, and Ray."

And then, as an afterthought, he added, "And . . . bless Mrs. Von Whistle."

Herbie turned off the light and crawled into bed. His dog nosed his way under the covers and put his chin on Herbie's chest. As they lay there, Herbie could see the streetlights shining through the big maple tree. It seemed quiet until he heard a neighbor call, "RYAN!"

Ryan was a teenager who lived up the street. His mother always called him at 9:00 to come home.

"COMING."

Herbie smiled. He was familiar with the sounds. He listened to the cars passing by. He heard a plane fly overhead. He heard his parents and Olivia walking around downstairs. At 9:30 P.M. the house became quiet. Herbie figured everyone was in bed, like himself.

Herbie was tired from being up late the night before with Raymond, so he dozed off to sleep. At 11:00 P.M. he woke up when he heard his dad backing out of the driveway. Herbie knew he was going to work at the airplane factory. Herbie wondered if his dad had closed the back door tightly. The wind often blew it open.

Herbie sat up and turned on the light by his bed. Did *he* remember to close the attic door? He didn't want any visits from a raccoon or water rat.

Herbie decided he had to see for himself. Quietly, he went over to the table and grabbed the flashlight. He didn't want to wake up his dog. He might bark and disturb his mother and sister. After Herbie closed the door to the little room securely behind him, he tiptoed across the attic floor. The flashlight made shadows everywhere. Herbie tried to look straight ahead at the yellow beam of light.

Herbie could feel his heart thumping loudly against his chest. Quickly, he ran down the stairs. No, he didn't close the attic door. It was ajar. When Herbie got down to the bottom of the stairs, he noticed the back door was open. The cool evening breeze was strong and made Herbie shiver in his cotton pajamas. Herbie closed the door tightly. They had to get a lock for that door, he thought.

Herbie breathed easier. Everything was secured now. As he walked back up the stairs and across the attic, he heard a growling sound.

"Hamburger Head?" Herbie replied. Quickly he shined the light on the little room. The door was still closed.

Herbie slowly inched his way back to the stairs. He didn't like the sound of that growl. It was high-pitched and mean.

Just as Herbie backed up toward the steps, he saw something big and hairy jump out of the shadows.

The *raccoon!* It was huge, Herbie thought. Its dark eyes were staring at Herbie. "GGrraauuugh chhheeeEE," it growled! This must be the same raccoon that got trapped inside Mrs. Von Whistle's hallway.

Herbie could feel perspiration dripping down his face, his hands were shaking, and his heart was racing. Slowly Herbie continued his retreat down the stairs. He didn't want to frighten the animal or make it angry.

The raccoon stood his ground while he watched Herbie descend the stairs. Two more steps to go, Herbie thought.

Suddenly the raccoon opened his mouth and showed his teeth.

Herbie was so nervous, his hands started shaking and he dropped the flashlight. Two D-cell batteries popped out and rolled down the stairway. Now he was frantically feeling around the door for the knob. His source of light was gone. It was pitch black. Where's that knob? Herbie thought.

The noises frightened the raccoon. He gristled back, "GGrraauuugh ChhheeeeeEE!"

Just as Herbie felt something hairy brush up against him, he found the knob.

Quickly he opened the door and closed it tightly behind him.

"WAHAAAaaaa!" the raccoon shrilled like a crying baby.

Herbie looked down. It's ring-tipped tail was caught in the door! Herbie's eyes started to fill up with water. He didn't want to hurt the raccoon, but he couldn't open the door. It might attack him.

"MOM!" he screamed at the top of his lungs.

Mrs. Jones sat up in bed. "HERBIE? WHERE ARE YOU?"

"IN THE HALLWAY!"

Mrs. Jones didn't bother to put on her slippers or grab her bathrobe. She just ran out into the hall in her blue flannel nightgown. "HER-BIE! What's the matter?"

As soon as she saw the tail in the attic door, she knew. "THE RACCOON!"

Olivia stood behind her mother. She was rubbing her eyes. "You're kidding!"

"The raccoon is caught against this door. Go call Mr. Hodgekiss, quick!"

Mrs. Jones ran to the phone. Olivia helped her brother hold the door. "Let me do this," she said. "We can't hurt him."

Very slowly, Olivia let the door open a crack.

"GRRrrrrrr!" The raccoon ran up the attic stairs and across the attic floor.

Herbie and Olivia leaned against the closed door.

"Ahhhh," Herbie sighed. "Thanks, Olive."

Olivia nodded.

"He's on his way," Mrs. Jones said as she dashed out of the kitchen.

"Good," Herbie replied. Then he listened. "That's Hamburger Head. He's barking."

Olivia's eyes bulged. "Is he in the attic too?"

Herbie nodded. "I left him up there in the little room. He's probably trying to get out now."

"Hurry up, Mr. Hodgekiss," Olivia said to herself.

Herbie listened to his dog's wild barking and scratching at the door. When the scratching became loud thuds, he knew his dog was throwing his body against the door. "He wants out! He smells that raccoon now."

When the backyard door slammed open, Herbie and Olivia jumped. "MR. HODGE-KISS! You're here!"

"I'm sure glad you two are okay. Is the raccoon in the attic?"

"Y-yes!" Herbie stammered. "I hope my dog doesn't get out of the little room."

Herbie looked at Mr. Hodgekiss's equipment. The large wire mesh box in his right hand reminded Herbie of a lobster trap. In his left hand was a pole about the size of a pool stick with a cable noose at one end.

"What's that?" he asked.

"My snare pole. I'll try to get the noose around the raccoon's head and shoulder. I can release the cable with this lock mechanism by the handle. See?"

Herbie looked.

"Now, you two go into the kitchen where it's safe. I'll take care of this."

Herbie was disappointed. He wanted to

watch Mr. Hodgekiss catch the raccoon.

As soon as they went inside the kitchen, they heard Mr. Hodgekiss's heavy footsteps go across the attic. Then they stopped. They heard barking and growling. Then a scuffle.

The next five minutes seemed like a lifetime to Herbie. Finally they heard footsteps going back across the attic to the stairwell. And then a knock at the kitchen door.

Herbie opened it right away and looked down at the box trap. The raccoon was inside, growling and clawing at the wire-mesh sides.

Herbie was glad the raccoon was caught. He didn't want him biting any more neighbors. But he also felt sorry for the animal. He belonged near a river with lots of trees, Herbie thought.

"I'll . . . take him to the health department early tomorrow morning to be tested. I'll let you know if he has rabies or not."

Herbie stood closer to his sister. The word rabies frightened Herbie.

"Thank you, Mr. Hodgekiss, so much for coming at this hour of night and helping us out," Mrs. Jones said.

"Well, I'm glad the neighborhood is safe again. It can be an awful worry," Mr. Hodgekiss replied. "I know Mrs. Von Whistle will be relieved too. 'Night, everyone."

"'Night," Herbie and Olivia replied.

Herbie watched Annabelle's father carry the box trap and snare pole down the steps. It was over. Finally.

Suddenly Herbie remembered Hamburger Head!

He ran upstairs, pulled the lightcord, and raced across the attic floor. As soon as he opened the door to the little room, his dog jumped on him, licking his face.

"Good boy," Herbie replied as he hugged his dog. "You stayed inside."

"Ruf! Ruf!" Hamburger Head wagged his tail back and forth.

Mrs. Jones stood at the top of the stairs. "Why don't you sleep downstairs tonight, Herbie?" she suggested.

Herbie liked the idea of sleeping in his own bed. It had been a scary night. But the threat of danger was over, and Herbie wanted to finish what he had started out to do.

"Thanks, Mom, but we'll be fine up here in the attic." Herbie grabbed his dog before he had a chance to run away. "'Night!"

"I'm real proud of you, Herbie," Mrs. Jones called.

Herbie smiled, then he went inside his little room with his dog.

13

Dad Returns

When Herbie opened his eyes the next morning, Mr. Jones was sitting on his bed.

"DAD!" Herbie exclaimed as he gave him a big hug. "You're home from work!"

Mr. Jones patted his son's back. "I'm so sorry you had to go through all that. I had no idea raccoons went up into attics."

Herbie looked around. "Where's Hamburger Head?"

"He raced out of here as soon as I opened the door. Speaking of doors, I'm putting a lock on our *backyard door* today."

"Thanks, Dad. I sure hope that raccoon doesn't have rabies. If he *isn't* rabid, Mrs. Von Whistle won't have to worry, and that raccoon

86

can go back to the river where he belongs."

"Herbie, I have to tell you something about rabies testing."

"What?"

"The lab has to take a specimen from the raccoon's brain, so . . . regardless whether or not he's rabid, he's going to die."

Herbie got out of bed and looked out the window. A squirrel was running up a branch of the maple tree. "That's so unfair, Dad." Herbie wiped his eyes with his sleeve.

"I know, son. But sometimes science *has* to take the life of an animal in order to improve the lives of humans."

Herbie turned around. His eyes were red. "When I'm older, *I'm going* to vet school, and I'm going to discover a test for rabies that *won't* kill innocent animals."

"Good," his dad replied.

Then they hugged like bears.

14

Friends in the Attic

That day after school, Herbie and his friends got together to work on their reading project. As they passed through the kitchen, on their way to the attic, there was a note on the table.

Dear Herbie,
Mr. Hodgekiss called.
He said to call him when
you get in. I'm going
back to bed.
                    Dad

Herbie picked up the phone and dialed Mr. Hodgekiss's number. His mother had it printed on their frequent-callers list next to the phone.

Everyone gathered around and waited to hear what Mr. Hodgekiss was telling Herbie. Annabelle had her head down. Margie and Sarah had their fingers crossed. Ray and Jose were trying to put their ears next to Herbie's.

As soon as Herbie hung up, he told them the good news. "The raccoon isn't rabid."

"YEA!" everyone cheered.

Except Annabelle.

"Aren't you happy for Mrs. Von Whistle and the raccoon?" Sarah asked.

Annabelle looked up. Tears were streaming down her face. Herbie knew why.

Margie immediately went over to her old friend. "What's the matter, Annabelle?"

"Once . . . in . . . a . . . while, m-my d-dad has to take an animal to be tested for rabies. When that happens . . . the animal is . . . k-k-killed."

Sarah covered her mouth.

Jose and Ray shook their heads.

Margie put her arm around Annabelle. "That's so sad."

"I try n-n-not to th-think about it," Annabelle said as she gasped for air.

Herbie looked at Annabelle. "Don't worry. I'm changing all that. When I go to vet school, I'm going to discover a new way to test for rabies that *won't* endanger the lives of animals."

Annabelle smiled at Herbie, then she took a daisy handkerchief out of her initialed handbag. "I wish we could do something now for that p-poor raccoon."

After she blew her nose, Margie had an idea. "We could make raccoon pictures just like we did in class."

Annabelle put her hanky away. "Let's do it! I have lots of drawing paper in my binder and colored pencils, too. Do you have some thumbtacks, Herbie?"

Herbie looked in the bottom kitchen drawer. "Right here."

The next twenty minutes the group sat at Herbie's kitchen table and drew raccoon pictures. No one said much, they were too busy

concentrating. When they were finished, Herbie and his friends raced upstairs and tacked their pictures on the wide wooden beams in the attic.

"It looks real nice," Sarah said.

Annabelle nodded. Then she walked over to Margie. "And so are you. I know why the librarian picked you to be her helper. Miss Pinkham probably told her how kind and helpful you are."

Margie smiled. "Thanks, Annabelle."

"Thank *you*, Margie, for being so understanding about my feelings. I don't deserve a friend like you."

Margie didn't say anything. She just gave Annabelle a big, long hug and Annabelle hugged her back.

Suddenly Ray bellowed, "Hey, Sarah, did you bring some eats?"

"Right here," she said, holding up a coffee canister.

"Let's start our meeting!" Ray said as he ran to the little room.

"Look at the pretty daisies!" Annabelle said

as she walked into Herbie's attic room. "And the beautiful view!"

"Look at the baby squirrel!" Margie squealed. "We should meet here often."

Herbie beamed. It made him feel good that his friends liked his room.

Ray looked behind the garbage can. "Haven't seen another raccoon visitor yet."

"They usually don't come out during the day," Annabelle snapped. "Dad told me the raccoon that Mrs. Von Whistle found in her hallway that morning was trapped from the night before."

Before Ray plopped down on the bed he checked underneath the bedspread. "Never can be too sure. Maybe one got trapped up here."

Annabelle rolled her eyeballs at Margie. "Most raccoons are just fine, Raymond! You don't have to be afraid of them."

Sarah held up a can of cookies. "Pass these Snickerdoodles around."

Annabelle quickly grabbed the can and put the lid back on the container. "Not here, Sarah.

We might get crumbs on the rug. Herbie just vacuumed."

Herbie raised his eyebrows. Hmmmm, he thought. She noticed that, too. Maybe I'll do the vacuuming myself next time.

"If we have a snack, we should go down to Herbie's kitchen," Annabelle advised.

Jose threw his hands in the air. "You're a fanatic about neatness, Annabelle!"

"That's it!" Herbie replied.

"What?" everyone said.

"I just got an idea for the name of our reading group. Fanatics!"

"FANATICS?"

"Fans of the attic. Get it?"

Everyone looked at Herbie. And then, one by one, they started to nod yes.

"It's distinctive," Annabelle said. "Of course, we will need to meet in the attic regularly. Once a week okay, Herbie?"

"I'll check with Dad."

Having friends in the attic made it seem more like home, Herbie thought.

"I'll tell Miss Pinkham the name of our group tomorrow," Annabelle said.

Herbie put his finger in the air. "Just a minute. We have to do something to make this official."

"What are you talking about?" Annabelle asked.

Herbie came back in the room with a can of purple paint and two brushes. "Dad said I could do some artwork on the walls if I wanted. I want you guys to write your names as official members of the Fanatics reading group."

Annabelle raised her eyebrows. "Are you *sure* it's okay to put graffiti on your walls?"

Ray jumped in. "I was there when his dad said it."

Annabelle took out her pocket dictionary. "Let's see," she said. "This says you're supposed to spell it f-a-n-a-t-i-c-s. But since we're fans of the attic, I'm going to spell it like this. Annabelle took out a brush and neatly printed FANATTICS across the side wall. Then she wrote "Annabelle" in cursive with a daisy at the end. Ray printed his name with large letters.

"Careful, you're dripping!" Annabelle said as she quickly gathered some old newspapers from around the corner and laid them down on the rug.

"What's that in your picture, dripping down from your mouth?" Margie asked.

Ray smiled. "BLOOD. This is Count Dracula!"

Annabelle made a face. "Raymond, I'm putting an X over 'blood.' That's gross."

When they were all finished painting and cleaning up, they stood back and admired their work.

"Now I think the Fanattics should get down to business," Annabelle said.

For the next hour the Fanattics wrote down the most interesting facts about the history of hamburgers on large yellow chart paper with Magic Markers. Raymond and Jose illustrated some of them.

"I'm making a diploma for Hamburger University," Jose said. "Just think, you can get a degree in Hamburgerology!"

"I'm drawing a cheeseburger with everything on it," Ray said.

Annabelle wrote in her best cursive hand-writing.

At 4:15 Herbie suggested they take a break. "Who wants to play hide-and-go-seek in my attic?"

Everyone but Annabelle raised a hand.

"Who's 'it'?" Sarah asked.

"I think Herbie should be 'it,'" Margie said. "It's his attic."

Herbie liked the sound of those words . . . his attic. "Okay, I'm closing my eyes. Goal is my bed. Ready, one . . . two . . . three . . . four . . ."

As Herbie counted, Ray, Annabelle, Margie, Jose, and Sarah raced out of his room and into the large attic. Each one found a secret hiding place, ducked down, and didn't say a word.

". . . nineteen . . . twenty. HERE I COME!" Herbie called.

As soon as Herbie stepped into the large attic room, he started searching for his friends. He couldn't remember when he actually looked at all the stuff that was stored up there. Now that the afternoon sun streamed in through the windows, Herbie could see why there were so many weird shadows at night.

He stopped and looked at some of his old toys next to Olivia's baby doll carriage. He spotted the boxes of Christmas tree ornaments, the racks of winter coats, the stacks of old board games, and big empty boxes that the washing machine and refrigerator had come in. He saw their camping equipment, the big tent, stove, lantern, and sleeping bags. Then he noticed the cobwebs above the stairway. The light from the window made them glisten like Christmas garlands. Herbie smiled when he spotted four spiders. They reminded him of his old pet spiders, Gus and Spike. He decided to give them names like the ones in *Charlotte's Web*. "You're Charlotte, Joy, Aranea, and Nellie."

Suddenly the attic seemed like a happy place to Herbie.

"FREE!" shouted Margie and Jose, tagging the bed.

"FREE!" shouted Annabelle, Ray, and Sarah.

Herbie ran back to his room. All his friends were laughing.

"You're too easily distracted," Sarah complained. "Let's go downstairs and eat my Snickerdoodle cookies."

"Yeah!" Jose and Ray replied.

As the group walked down to the kitchen, Herbie hesitated.

"Come on!" Ray called. "My stomach's growling."

Herbie took one last look around the attic and smiled. There was Hamburger Head by the sunny window, sleeping with all four legs in the air. Herbie listened to his dog snore as the lacy curtains billowed in the breeze and gently tickled the dog's paws.

For some reason Herbie knew he wouldn't have trouble sleeping in the attic anymore.